# The Wish

For some grown-ups, having a child to love is the most wondrous gift life can give. For some, it is the very meaning of life itself.

Flora's cherished dream of having a child to call her own, had never come true. As the years passed and her hopes faded, Flora poured all her love into the garden of her small terraced house. She nurtured trees, flowers, and vegetables with a mother's loving and tender care. Sometimes she would talk to them, telling them how proud she was of their beautiful blooms. Other times, as she watered, she would whisper words of encouragement softly, telling her plants to try and be the very best they could be. Words she longed to tell to a child.

Working in the garden, growing produce to sell, kept her busy and mostly happy. But there were some darker days, when every flower in the world could not fill the hole in Flora's heart. No matter how hard she dug the earth or ripped weeds from the borders, she could not wither the sadness that grew in her. One April morning, despite the bright sunshine, despair crawled like poison ivy and curled tightly around her heart.

In the centre of Flora's garden stood a magnificent cherry blossom tree with clouds of exquisite pink blooms, making it look like a giant stick of candy floss. The delicate flowers on its proud branches swayed in the fresh, spring breeze, and thousands of petals fell like confetti, scattering themselves along the stone path that ran around the tree.

Flora grabbed a brush and began to sweep at them as hard as she could, her eyes filling with hot tears. She poured her dream into every stroke.

'I wish I had a child,' she whispered.

A cloud of petals flew high into the air, dancing in the sky. Flora felt a wind begin to blow, whipping up more of the fallen blossom. Another, more powerful stroke of the brush.

'I wish for a child!' Flora spoke louder now.

Petals soared again. A strong gust blew more from the branches and they waltzed frenziedly together in the air around her. Flora summoned all her strength and swept a mountain of petals higher.

'I wish for a child!' she called out to the wind.

A storm of blossom petals circled faster in sky, a pale pink tornado surging in front of her. What was happening? Flora staggered back, falling to the ground. As she stared at the whirling cloud, she noticed something starting to appear. It was a face. A woman's face, shaped into the hurricane of petals.

Flora gasped.

'You wished for a child Flora.'

The blossom was speaking to her! Flora drew her breath and nodded, barely able to believe what was happening.

'It's all I have ever wished for.'

'Your faith is almost lost, but don't despair.'

Flora shook her head. 'It can never happen now…'

'You will have a daughter, Flora. She will be a gift, a magical child. But for her to stay with you as a real girl, she must earn her place in the world. She will face tests. She must be kind, honest and strong. If she fails, she will return to the garden and to me, and will be blossom once again. Do you accept?'

Flora's heart leapt. Could she really have a child to call her own?

'Yes! Yes, of course, anything! Thank you! Thank you so much!'

The blossom smiled gently. Then the wind blew hard again, and the face became blurred, dissolving into the blizzard of petals. Faster and faster they raced, surrounding Flora, making her feel faint and dizzy. She could hardly see, everything was a pink storm.

Suddenly the wind sucked the petals high into the sky. They hung there, and all went still.

Then the petals began to fall gently. But they did not scatter randomly. They flew down deliberately, each with its own purpose, each to a precise point, each had its place. With every one, a form was taking shape. Flora saw feet being built, petals became legs, melting into each other to create almost translucent skin, which glistened like the first morning dew. They moulded arms, sculpted a neck. Then Flora saw them casting the features of a young girl's face, falling to create soft, puffed pink hair. Curls like fluffy bunches of blossom swayed down past her shoulders. In one final blast, the petals swirled and fashioned a plain pink dress that draped around her.

Flora gasped at the vision of the flower girl in front of her. Slowly, the magical child opened her eyes. They were bright, leaf green and sparkling with life. Sunshine filled the garden and her flower-bud lips burst into a glorious smile.

'Hi Mum. I'm Cherry.'

# Alive

Cherry could barely believe it. She was alive! She bounded over to Flora, gave her a huge hug, then jumped back and breathed in the heavenly scent of the flowering garden.

Her excited eyes darted around. She saw a sea of bluebells, their heads nodding at her happily. There were brightly coloured tulips, pastel-coloured sweet peas climbing high, huge peonies like cheerleaders' pom-poms, long-stemmed stocks topped with bunches of fragrant petals, earthy beds full of purple, yellow and white freesias. Their heady scents all mingled in the air, the sweetest of nature's perfumes.

The garden, though as narrow as the house, stretched back a surprisingly long way and the far end was devoted to vegetables. There were neat rows of sumptuous cabbages, crunchy kale, crisp lettuces, dark velvet-green spinach, broccoli, peas, onions, carrots, parsnips and turnips. But the centrepiece of the garden, dividing the two areas and standing proud, like a queen overlooking her subjects, was the mighty blossom tree.

'It's sooooo beautiful!' exclaimed
Cherry as she ran whooping at full
pelt up the stone path, whizzing past
flower beds, occasionally skidding to
a sudden stop to bury her head into
some blooms to smell them. She threw
her arms out and spun around, looking
into the sky, feeling the sun on her face for
the first time.

'Whoooooohoooooo! This is
aaaaa-mmmaaazzzzingg! What shall

we do now Mum, what shall we do? I'm soooooo excited!' Cherry could not stop bouncing up and down.

Flora was laughing with tears of wonder in her eyes. This magical flower girl, bursting with joy and happiness was hers to love.

'Let's go inside and settle you in. The house is small Cherry, I don't have much, but...'

Cherry had rushed ahead and into the house.

'It's so cute Mum! I love it already!' she shouted from inside.

Cherry really did love it too. The front door opened straight into a small living room. It had a low ceiling which instantly made it feel homely and cosy. On the left of the room was an open fire. Opposite, a sofa and armchair were crammed in. The furniture was tired and worn, the rose print was faded, but it looked welcoming and comfortable. Cherry flopped backwards and stretched out, beaming. Yep, this was home.

To the back of the room was a door that was slightly open. Cherry could see kitchen units painted a pale moss green. There were small piles of mismatched china plates and bowls on open shelves, a few cups and a small teapot. It was clean and quaint. Her mum may be poor but she had made her house as pretty as could be.

'So Cherry, you are going to need a bedroom!'

'I get my own bedroom?' Cherry exclaimed.

'Well, I wouldn't get too excited, it's possibly the smallest room you've ever seen, but yes, it's yours!'

'Whooooaaah! That's awesome Mum!' Cherry was up off the sofa in a flash to hug Flora. 'Let's go! C'mon Mum! Let's see it!'

Just behind the sofa, was a wooden staircase. Within seconds, Cherry was skipping up the stairs two at a time with Flora trotting behind her trying to keep up. At the top, were three doors.

'This is my room,' said Flora, revealing a simple room with wooden floorboards, thin muslin curtains at the window and a bed made up with fresh white sheets. At her bedside, a small vase of sweet peas picked from the garden sat next to a brass lamp. On a clothes rail in the corner, hung two chunky hand-knitted jumpers and three dresses which Flora would wear in rotation. They were each made of firm cotton, simple in shape, but around the neck, hem and sleeve of every one was detailed embroidery. A chain of daisies circled one, bouquets of roses dotted around another, and boughs of blossom the third.

'It's lovely Mum,' Cherry said gently.

Flora bustled on. 'The bathroom…'

She opened and shut the door quickly, just long enough for Cherry to spot a basic tub and basin.

'And this…' said Flora timidly but looking rather excited, 'is your room…' She opened the door slowly and gestured for Cherry to go in.

Cherry drew her breath. The room was tiny. White curtains waved a welcome to her at the open window. There was just enough space for a single bed and a table next to it. A patchwork quilt of all kinds of different and colourful fabric was spread smoothly across the bed and a fat, feathery pillow rested on a painted wooden headboard, plumped up, just waiting for a tired head to sink into it.

Cherry ran her hands over the quilt, examining each square. There were so many different patterns! Multi-coloured spots, stripes, zigzags, rainbow swirls, florals, checks. To Cherry it was the most wonderful, crazy, quirky, mishmash of material that came together just perfectly.

Flora was watching, a little colour rising to her cheeks, 'I collect the material, most of it from old clothes people are throwing out, and I make quilts and sell them at the market. This is the first one I made though, so it's a special one.'

'No way Mum, I can't believe you made it, it's amazing!' Cherry felt all the tiny stitches her mother had sewn.

'I always hoped someone would love it!' beamed Flora.

'I totally LOVE it, thanks Mum. Seriously, best bedroom EVER!'

A loud rumble startled them both. Cherry looked panicked. 'What was that?!'

Her mum was laughing, 'That was your tummy! Let's have some supper, and while we eat,' her face clouded over a little, 'there's something important I have to tell you.'

'Sure Mum,' said Cherry lightly.

As she followed her mother out of the bedroom, she passed a carved wooden mirror on the wall and caught sight of herself for the first time. She stopped abruptly, startled by her own appearance. She looked so different from her mother, who had long, straight dark hair, chocolate-coloured eyes and tanned, golden skin from all her time spent outside in the garden.

Cherry's hair was pink! It was as if bunches and bunches of the blossom had been gathered up and placed all around her head. She reached up to touch the cloud of pastel curls. They were softer than she expected. As she ran her hands through their length, petals scattered from the tips, and floated around her, dancing in the air like butterflies.

She blinked bark-brown eyelashes and peered closer to the mirror. The green of her eyes made her think of the garden outside, where she had come from. She heard her mother call her downstairs and took one last glance in the mirror. Her eyes flickered. Did she look different to everyone else she wondered? She didn't want to be different. She wanted to be the same, to fit in.

A dark feeling suddenly swept over her but Cherry shrugged it off and smiled at the bubblegum-haired girl in the mirror. She smiled back and Cherry skipped downstairs, wondering what was the important something her mum needed to say.

# The Warning

Cherry sat on the sofa, tucking into the most delicious stew.

'The vegetables are from the garden, cooked the old-fashioned way,' winked Flora.

A little black pot was hanging over the fire, bubbling away. Luckily, Flora's garden seemed to produce mountains of vegetables, enough to supply the stall she ran at the weekly market, with plenty left over for her too.

She made posies of flowers wrapped in brown paper and tied with string and sold cuttings from her plants, hoping other people would love to grow them. As well as the patchwork quilts on offer, she embroidered tablecloths and napkins for customers to buy too. All together, it made her enough money to scrape by.

Cherry took a big slurp of stew, dribbling quite a bit of it down her chin. 'Mmmmmm,' she gurgled.

'Cherry,' her mother paused, 'do you like it here?'

'I goo! I weewee goo! Wove it!' Cherry's mouth was full again and the words weren't coming out quite right.

Flora couldn't help but laugh. 'But for you to stay Cherry,' her mum was suddenly serious again, 'you need to be kind, honest and strong. You know what's right in your heart and you must always listen to it. It won't always be easy, it's hard for us all. But for us to be together, for you to have this life, you must try.'

'Sure Mum,' shrugged Cherry, shovelling more stew into her hungry mouth, 'kind, honest and strong. Got it.'

'Ouch!' her mother cried out. The fire had spat

glowing embers onto the old tapestry rug, one had landed on Flora too. She swiped at them with the tea towel she had been holding. 'That fire has a mind of its own!'

'You ok Mum?'

'I'm fine,' she said, swatting at tiny rogue flames, 'promise me now Cherry? Deep down, you'll know what's right.'

'Yup, promise. Abbbbb-sollllll-utely!'

Cherry could see her mum looked a little bit frustrated. But she totally got it. Be kind. Be honest. Be strong. Not hard.

'So, tomorrow…' dramatic pause from her mum, happy now the fire was behaving.

'Yes…?'

'You're going to…' another dramatic pause.

'Yes…?'

'SCHOOL!'

Cherry nearly choked on her last spoonful.

'YES!' said Cherry, jumping up. She bounded onto the sofa and started jumping up and down, the occasional petal shaking from her hair.

She sprung down to the floor to hug her mother. She would make friends, learn about stuff, it was going to be the best!

'Thanks Mum, it'll be amazing and I'll be so good, I promise! Ok, I'm going to bed so I can be totally ready! Night Mum, love you.'

Cherry skipped up the stairs and burst into her bedroom. There it was again. The mirror. Its frame had been painstakingly carved with delicate flowers and butterflies, and at the four corners were swallows in flight. It must have been her mother's work. As she stopped to take a closer look, smiling at how lifelike each flower was, Cherry saw her shining eyes reflecting back at her, full of expectation.

She was going to school just like a real girl! She'd have friends, she'd learn, have fun. She shook her head barely believing how lucky she was, and watched in wonder as petals began dancing out from the tips of her hair again, as excited as she was. They skipped up around her pink curls, jiggling and bouncing in the air. Cherry giggled at the impatient petals who clearly couldn't wait to get to school either.

She reached out and traced her fingers across the oak frame of the mirror, feeling a connection with the wood and nature. She glanced out of the window at the blossom tree. It swayed gently and sent a posy of glittering petals high on the evening breeze towards her window. Cherry's heart lifted with them. They floated through the window and circled around her, joining the petal party fluttering around her hair.

Suddenly a pair of petals landed on the tip of her nose. Cherry's eyes widened. They weren't petals at all. They were wings. A tiny pink butterfly was staring at her with huge eyes. Somehow, it seemed to be smiling.

'Hello you,' whispered Cherry softly, not wanting to startle it.

The butterfly blinked, tilted its head to one side and wiggled a wing at her as a little wave and gave her nose a tickle with one of its legs. It seemed to be smiling even more. Cherry giggled.

'Well, what's your name then? Are you going to be my first friend?'

The butterfly spun around excitedly.

'I'll take that as a yes,' she laughed, 'so you'll need a name. Hmm. What about… Bella? Bella the butterfly?'

The butterfly shook its head firmly.

'Briony? Billy? Bethan? Bruce? Belinda?'

It rolled its eyes.

'Betsan? Ben? Brian? Bob?'

The butterfly was starting to look rather cross. It frowned hard, straightened its antennae haughtily and tucked its wings firmly behind it. Then it folded its legs as if putting its hands on its hips.

'Ok, ok. Let me think. The perfect name for a best buddy… Wait! That's it! Buddy, Bud for short. You flew from the blossom buds like me too, so Bud suits you just perfectly!'

The butterfly nodded proudly. Looking very pleased indeed, Bud flew to the side of Cherry's cheek and fluttered his wings softly against her,

giving her a gentle butterfly kiss. Then he took off and perched on top of her head, nestling in comfortably.

Cherry looked back in the mirror and beamed at Bud who beamed right back. He was exactly the same colour as her pink hair. If she hadn't known he was there, she'd never have spotted him. He wiggled his wing, waved a leg to say goodnight, yawned, then disappeared down into her curls.

'Looks like you've found a new home Bud, just like me. Sleep tight, sweet dreams.'

Cherry pulled back the patchwork quilt and climbed into her bed. She let her head sink deeply into the pillow and closed her eyes. She couldn't wait to go to school tomorrow, and she already had a friend to go with her.

# School

Cherry was half-skipping, half-running ahead of her mum on the path in the park. She had a slice of crusty brown bread smothered in butter and home-made raspberry jam in her hand that she was wolfing down on the way. Bud flew alongside her, his antennae alert, focusing intently on their mission to get to school.

'Here we go, Bud, big day.' Cherry's mouth was full and there were a number of crumbs stuck on her chin.

Bud frowned and dabbed delicately at his own mouth with his leg as he flew.

'Got it,' Cherry wiped her face with the back of her hand, 'thanks Bud.'

He gave her a quick wink before turning his attention back to the serious business of the journey to school. He had to get them there on time and looking smart on their first day.

Flora was trying to keep up with Cherry, who was skipping ahead. Flora had butterflies in her tummy. What if her daughter's first day didn't go well? What if Cherry didn't make any friends? What if…? Flora shook herself. It would all be fine. It had to be.

'Hurry up Mum!'

It was only a short walk from the house to get to school, through Larksbridge Park and along the street of the market town, but for Cherry, it felt like it had taken forever.

They were at the school gates at last. Cherry was hopping from foot to foot with excitement, as if the pavement was on fire and she couldn't stand still on it.

'You must be Cherry?' said a booming voice behind her.

Cherry jumped and spun around. Bud dived

into her hair and hid. An enormous woman, with short, cropped coal-black hair, small eyes and a wide smiling mouth was standing over her.

'Welcome to Eden's Gate Primary. I'm the head, Miss Turner, and don't think I don't know they all call me Turnip! It's this thing I think.' She tapped a large, knobbly nose that protruded magnificently from her otherwise rather flat face. Cherry could see a very clear resemblance to a fresh turnip that sat in the vegetable basket in the kitchen and she didn't know quite what to say, but Miss Turner seemed to find it all very funny.

'You must be Flora.' Miss Turner held out a huge hand to Flora for her to shake. Flora winced at Miss Turner's iron grip.

'Yes. Thank you so much Miss Turnip. Turner! I mean Miss Turner, for taking Cherry at such short notice.'

'Delighted!' bellowed the head. Although Cherry saw her eyes quickly dart up to her flamingo-pink hair, but Miss Turner said nothing.

'We have a second-hand uniform all ready

which should be just your size. Follow me Cherry, quick change and it's time for class. Good timing too, it's art this morning. Come along. 3.30 prompt pick-up Flora.'

'Good luck!' Flora felt her heart squeeze as she quickly gave Cherry a kiss.

'Mum!' Cherry hoped none of the other kids had seen, so embarrassing, but Cherry was smiling. She knew how much her mum loved her and it gave her a spring in her step. With a quick wave, Cherry rushed after Miss Turner who was striding like a giant into the school. She seemed really nice – for a head teacher – but there was something about her that made Cherry think she never, ever wanted to make her cross.

Miss Turner burst into the classroom of Year 6, grabbing Cherry by the arm and thrusting her in front of everyone.

'New girl everyone!' Miss Turner blasted, 'this is Cherry, make her welcome.' Then she turned on her heels and flounced out of the door, slamming it behind her. Cherry took a deep breath.

'Hi.' Everyone in the class was staring at her. She thought of her own reflection, and looked around the class. She was aware how different she looked to everyone else in the room. She felt Bud stir in her hair, letting her know he was there and on her side. Cherry tried to smile at the class, but she caught some of the girls whispering, nudging each other, looking strangely at her. Were some of them laughing behind their hands? Suddenly she felt very self-conscious.

Cherry looked at the floor to try and escape their stares and block out the muttering. She felt a hot wave spread from her feet, right to her cheeks, which were now burning fuchsia pink. She just wanted to run straight back out of the door and go home. She had been so excited about starting school, she hadn't expected to feel like this.

'Quiet class!' hissed the teacher. Still Cherry could not look up. 'I'm Mrs Hemlock. Sit. Immediately.' She pointed. 'Next to Ruth.'

Cherry sat down as fast as she could. She took a deep breath and turned to look at Ruth.

The girl next to her grinned. Cherry felt a surge of relief and gave her a big smile back.

'Hi. Hemlock is strict,' Ruth whispered, 'really strict. Better not talk just yet, it will only mean trouble. Later at breaktime?'

Cherry nodded quickly. Ruth smiled again and carried on with her drawing. Cherry felt she had immediately made a friend. Ruth had a spectacular Afro like a bubble on her head, small round glasses and one of the loveliest smiles Cherry had ever seen. She turned and glanced around. Everyone else was still staring at her.

A girl sitting in the row in front nodded at her and smiled a cool smile. Her hair was cut in a sharp, sleek brown bob, her lips were full and shiny, curling at the sides, and her cat-like eyes glinted. The girl next to her nodded at Cherry too. Her auburn hair was cut in the exact same shape as her friend's. She had a smattering of freckles and icy blue eyes.

'Concentrate!' snapped Hemlock. Totally in synch, the girls turned their heads back to the teacher.

'Wow. They look pretty cool,' whispered Cherry.

Ruth snorted, 'They think they are. Tiffany and Amelia.' She shook her head. 'Wait, is something moving in your hair?'

Cherry didn't know what to say. How could she explain that a butterfly with attitude seemed to have taken up residence in her blossom curls. Before she had chance to reply, Mrs Hemlock slammed down her own sketchbook. Her face was grey and thin with strands of lank, greasy, hair hanging around it.

'Out! Out all of you! Ten minutes in the playground. Get this nonsense out of your system, then back in when you can actually focus on your work. Out of my sight!'

Ruth was right. Mrs Hemlock really was strict and in a massively bad mood by the looks of things. Everyone made a bolt for the classroom door, throwing nervous, suspicious glances her way, whispering to each other as they did. Cherry had dreamed that her classmates would all be coming up to say hello, wanting to make friends.

Now, the absolute opposite was happening.

Cherry swallowed hard. At least Ruth seemed friendly. She was quietly packing away her drawing pencils, in no rush to get out into the playground. Cherry looked up. The two cool girls who'd acknowledged Cherry earlier, were standing in front of her desk, both their heads cocked to the side at exactly the same angle as they looked Cherry up and down, assessing her from head to toe. Bud peeped out at them from Cherry's hair and frowned.

'What's with this look?' Tiffany waved her finger in Cherry's general direction.

'I… I don't know what you mean,' stammered Cherry, colour rising to her cheeks again.

'Like sure you don't. You do know you dyed your hair pink, right?' Amelia sniggered.

'I haven't, it's just the way my hair…' Cherry touched her hair self-consciously. She desperately hoped no petals would flutter out and that they wouldn't spot that a butterfly had made its home in her hair. The last thing she wanted was to draw any more attention to herself.

Tiffany and Amelia studied her again for what seemed to be an age. Tiffany spoke first.

'We don't mind if you dyed your hair. We like breaking rules.'

'But I didn't…'

'Coming with us? I'm Tiffany,' said the one with the dark bob.

'I'm Amelia,' said the other, 'I've got gum.'

'And I've got lip gloss,' said Tiffany.

'We can just like, hang out?'

Cherry felt a sudden rush of gratitude. These girls wanted to be her friends!

'Thanks!' gushed Cherry 'Shall we go Ruth?'

She glanced around at Ruth who seemed to be taking her time.

'Don't wait for her, she always takes ages.'

Cherry glanced back at Ruth, unsure.

'I love your hair,' said Tiffany. 'I want to dye mine pale blue. Maybe lilac.'

'I want pink hair like hers,' said Amelia. 'Come on, let's go!'

Cherry glowed.

'It's ok,' said Ruth without looking up.

'Really?' said Cherry hesitantly, 'I'll see you out there?'

Tiffany grabbed her arm a little too tightly. 'Let's go. We haven't got all day!' Tiffany looked around pointedly at Ruth.

'She's so slow,' muttered Amelia. 'Come with us Cherry. It'll be like, awesome.'

They linked arms with her and swaggered out of the classroom.

'We're going to be best friends,' whispered Tiffany, 'because we're the prettiest and coolest girls in the class.'

Cherry couldn't believe these girls wanted to be friends with her! She was in their gang already! She tried to glance back to see Ruth. Why was she taking so long? Well, she'd see her in the playground. These girls were really fun. She could chat to Ruth another time. School was amazing!

 # Break

Tiffany, Amelia and Cherry were sitting on a bench in the corner of the playground. Amelia had given Cherry strawberry-flavour gum. Now Tiffany had pulled out her swanky, new mobile phone.

'Let's take a selfie and post it. Lip gloss on girls!' And she whipped a sparkly tube out of her pocket.

Cherry wasn't entirely sure what a selfie was, everything was so new to her, but she was too embarrassed to say. The girls were plastering shiny pink gloss all over their lips.

'Your turn,' said Tiffany and she put some gloss on Cherry too. It tasted delicious.

'Ok, strike a pose girls!'

Tiffany held up her phone. Tiffany and Amelia were pouting their lips and looking up through their eyelashes. Cherry thought they looked a little bit ridiculous, but she was so desperate to fit in, she did the same even though she felt strange and uncomfortable. She felt Bud flutter in her hair. By contrast the little butterfly seemed to want to be part of this performance. He popped up to stretch his wings for the camera and flash his most dazzling smile.

Click! Click! Click! Click! The phone whirred.

Bud was so small and so well camouflaged that luckily, the girls didn't notice him, but Cherry could feel him shifting into different positions, posing for the shots, clearly loving a camera. Cherry tossed her head to warn him to lie low, and after one final wing flex, grudgingly, Bud crawled slowly back down into her curls.

'Ok, let's put some awesome filters on. Hashtag gorgeous. Hashtag besties. Hashtag the coolest. Hashtag Slick Girls. Secret handshake? Watch this Cherry!'

Their hands moved so fast, slapping palms, bumping fists, wiggling fingers and all the time they chanted,

*'We are the coolest*
*We are the best*
*We're The Slick Girl Gang*
*And we're better than the rest!'*

They finished by high fiving each other, a quick spin on the spot, ending with a pose, hands on hips and a pout. Cherry had never seen anything like it. So this is what the cool girls did?

'Errr... Awesome...' she said. She'd never used the word before but it seemed to be what Tiffany and Amelia said.

'I know, right?' said Tiffany. 'We're just sooooo...'

'SLICK!' they said in unison, and high fived again.

'We'll teach you the routine, now that you're in the gang too.'

'Thanks!' said Cherry excitedly. She couldn't believe her luck.

Out of the corner of her eye she saw Ruth. She was walking with a limp. Her left leg was bent and looked locked at the knee, her foot turned in slightly. A scruffy boy with tufty, short brown hair walked slowly next to her. Cherry watched them for a moment, chatting and laughing. Cherry felt her heart pull. She would go and join them.

'Ok. The Slick Girl's handshake! It's a shake, pull back, link fingers…' said Tiffany.

'I'm just going to go and say hello to Ruth a moment.'

'Cherry,' said Amelia crossly, 'don't you want to be in our gang?'

'Yes, of course! It's just…' she glanced over again to Ruth and the boy.

'Well then, you need to know the secret handshake, come on!'

'Ok. Sure,' said Cherry, not understanding why she felt so uneasy.

'Like O-M-S!' said Tiffany dramatically.

'That's Oh My Slick, so you know,' said Amelia.

'We've had thirty-two likes on our picture already! We are just so totally popular now. Everyone is loving you, asking who you are and saying how slick your hair is!'

'Really?' said Cherry breathlessly.

'The Slick Girls are famous! High five Cherry!' They all high fived.

Cherry was glowing. People liked her! She was

popular and in the Slick Girl Gang! Everything was working out. So why did she keep feeling this strange churning deep down?

# Mirror

Back in the classroom, Cherry sat next to Ruth again, who was busy sketching.

'Today, we are drawing things that make us happy,' said Mrs Hemlock through clenched teeth. She wasn't keen on children, but she did like bossing people about. 'Use your imaginations. Sketch whatever you want, but it must mean happiness to you.'

'What are you drawing Ruth?' whispered Cherry.

'A rose.' Ruth didn't seem as friendly as she had been earlier.

'Really? Why?'

'I love roses. Flowers. Nature. It always makes me happy.'

'Me too. Can I see?'

A little shyly, Ruth slid her paper towards Cherry. Bud crawled out from behind Cherry's ear to have a look.

'It's not finished or anything…'

'Wow! That's beautiful!' Cherry stared at the detail of the pencil sketch. 'It's so good, the rose actually looks real!'

Bud was looking at it and thinking how he'd love to drink some nectar from a flower like that.

Yum.

'Do you think so? Thanks, Cherry.' Ruth looked pleased and seemed much more friendly again.

Bud began to crawl back into his home, and Cherry saw Ruth's eyes dart towards him. Did she see him?

'Cherry, I think you have something in your…'

Cherry jumped in and changed the subject quickly. 'Ruth, can I ask what happened to your leg?'

'Oh there were some problems when I was
born, so it's always been like that. It just means I
walk more slowly, I can't really run very well and
sometimes it's hard for me to do fiddly things with
two hands, but it's fine,' she smiled.

'And who is the boy you were with?' Cherry

turned around. She saw him sat at the back of the class, concentrating on his drawing.

'It's Joe. He lives on the same street as me. We've known each other since we were three. He's my best friend.'

'I could tell. He seems…'

'CHERRY!' She jumped as Mrs Hemlock shouted her name. 'Talking. Talking. Talking. It seems our new girl has no manners whatsoever. Let me see your drawing!'

'I… I haven't started it yet,' stammered Cherry.

'Not. Even. Started.' Hemlock looked furious, 'And if you do ever decide to pick up a pencil, what might you be drawing?' she drawled.

Cherry frantically searched her mind for something. Happiness. Think, think. She had been happy last night, watching her petals dance around her in the wooden mirror her mother had carved, watching Bud as he snuggled into her hair.

'My mirror,' she smiled.

'A *mirror*?' Hemlock sneered.

'It has swallows on it and my Mum…' But before

she could finish explaining, some of the class started snickering. Cherry tried again. 'I was watching the reflection of the petals from the cherry tree and...'

The smothered laughter was spreading and now everyone was looking at her again. Even Ruth was studying her strangely.

'And why would a mirror make you happy Cherry? Because it would show your reflection and that hair of yours?' said Mrs Hemlock coldly.

'No! Not that! That's not what I meant at all! I meant...'

But it was too late. The class was erupting and Hemlock let them jeer a little longer before silencing them.

'I think we know exactly what you mean, Cherry. Maybe you should spend a little less time looking in the mirror. And by the way, dying your hair is against school policy. You'll have to change that as soon as you can,' she said coldly.

'But this is my...'

'Anyone else have drawings to share?' Hemlock interrupted.

'I've drawn Tiffany,' said Amelia.

'And I've drawn Amelia,' said Tiffany.

'It's slick!' they said in unison and high fived again.

'Wait!' Amelia lunged at Tiffany's drawing. 'I do NOT look like that!' she yelled. 'You've given me a goat face!'

'And you've made me look like a witch!' shrieked Tiffany.

They started screeching like demented cats, howling and clawing at each other's unflattering portraits.

Cherry ignored the commotion and sat miserably. She hung her head, letting her hair fall forward to hide her face. They weren't giving her a chance. It was so unfair. She felt Bud in her hair stroking her softly. Her eyes began to prickle strangely, and then, not tears, but petals began to fall, fluttering onto her lap. One after another they floated down quietly, as the chaos continued in the classroom around her.

'It wasn't what I meant,' she whispered under

her breath, 'it wasn't, it wasn't…'

But nobody heard her. Nobody saw her petal tears. Nobody, except Ruth.

# The Tree

When the bell rang at the end of the day, Cherry sprinted out of school. She saw Flora waiting in the yard. Cherry felt petal tears in her eyes again as she saw her mum. Please not here, not now, she thought.

'Can we just go, Mum, quick!'

Flora hugged her briefly, clasped her hand and they walked briskly out of the schoolyard.

'I know something happened today Cherry. What was it?'

'How did you know?' Cherry suddenly felt so ashamed, she could barely look at her mum.

'You'll see when we get home. Can you tell me?'

Cherry took a deep breath. It was so hard to say it out loud, but then everything came tumbling out.

'I said something but it all got twisted around and I didn't mean it at all, but everyone was laughing. Then there were these girls who were really nice to me, but they were showing off and I did too. I should have waited for my new friend Ruth, who is really lovely, but I didn't. That wasn't kind was it? I did everything wrong Mum!'

Cherry gulped and this time could not stop the petal tears from falling.

She was so confused by everything. Why was it so hard to make the right choices sometimes? To do the right thing?

Her petal tears floated sadly around her. Bud swooped sorrowfully with them.

'It's ok Cherry. Don't cry.' Flora squeezed her hand.

They arrived at the house and Cherry gasped when she saw the blossom tree. All the branches had drooped and sagged. The tree that had been in spectacular bloom only that morning, now looked sad and drained, its flowers starting to wilt. She felt Bud fly from her hair and saw him settle sadly on one of the limp branches.

'What's happened to it Mum?'

'I'm not absolutely sure,' said Flora, 'but you are being tested Cherry. Remember you need to be kind, honest and strong always. I think if you're not, well, the tree feels it. Did you say you weren't kind to Ruth? I think that makes the tree sad.'

Cherry looked at the forlorn tree. Faded petals fell from it.

'I think it's crying with you Cherry,' whispered Flora.

'What happens if I make any more mistakes? What happens then?'

'Let's not think about that. You just need to keep trying your best Cherry. Listen to your heart and it will all work out. I know it will.' But Flora swallowed hard. She could not bear to think of the tree's warning that if Cherry failed, she would disappear into the blossom again and would be lost to her forever.

Cherry gulped, 'I was trying to fit in. I just wanted them all to like me and… I feel so different to everyone else.'

She hugged her mother as tight as she could. Her petal tears drifted into the air and merged with those from the weeping cherry tree. Bud flew from the tree to join their solemn gathering. Petals fell like tender rain around Cherry and Flora as they held each other.

'I'm sorry. I'll do better tomorrow Mum, I promise,' she whispered.

Flora gave her a final, tight squeeze.

'Come on. I've got a treat for you that's just about ready. Prepare yourself for Flora's Fabulous Crumble! Made with fresh rhubarb picked today.'

Flora pulled an iron dish out of the oven and Cherry felt her mouth water at the sight and smell of the golden, buttery crumb. It had crisped perfectly on top and bubbling pink rhubarb broke through around the edges.

Cherry sank into the sofa, hugging a generous helping in a steaming, comforting bowl. She took a large spoonful to her mouth, blew on it for a few seconds to cool it, then closed her eyes as she let the sweet crumble and sharp rhubarb dance on her tastebuds.

She began to feel better immediately.

Flora's heart tightened as she watched Cherry tucking in. She was relieved to see her looking happier and felt a small swell of pride that her cooking had helped. But a little crumble wasn't going to cure everything. She looked up from Cherry to the forlorn blossom tree and felt a stab of fear. Cherry had to find her way. Flora couldn't bear to lose her now.

# Gamers

It took all of Cherry's courage to walk into school the next day. She wanted to show everyone that she wasn't a vain girl who liked looking in mirrors and taking selfies, though she understood why everyone in the class probably thought that. Most of all, she wanted to prove to Ruth that she could be a kind and supportive friend.

Bud flew out from her hair, hovered in front of her face and gave her a firm stare.

'I know, Bud. I'll sort this, I promise.'

Cherry sighed and hung her head, but Bud was determined to cheer her up. He started darting and weaving in front of her, grinning wildly and wiggling his wings. Then he began hopping back and forth in the air like he was dancing to an imaginary song, eyes wide, willing her to join in.

'Bud, what on earth are you doing?'

He looked ridiculous and Cherry burst out laughing. Bud kept his moves going and soon Cherry was bouncing along to the butterfly's beat.

She began chanting.

*'Fly, fly*
*Little Buddy Butterfly*
*Look at those wings*
*Look at how they take you high*

*Fly, fly*
*Little Buddy Butterfly*
*You make me smile*
*You make me wanna reach the sky*

*Fly, fly*
*Little Buddy Butterfly*
*You're my best friend*
*You'll always be my wing guy!'*

Cherry whooped and Bud landed on the tip of her nose and took a bow.

'Thanks Bud. You know how to cheer me up, don't you?'

Bud looked smug and fluttered happily back up into her hair. His work was done.

With an extra spring in her step, Cherry was even more determined to put things right, starting with Ruth. She was so ashamed that she'd let herself get caught up with the Slick Girls and abandoned her. She would never make that mistake again.

Cherry saw Ruth sitting with Joe in the playground. The Slick Girls were flicking their hair, about to start taking selfies again. They spotted her immediately.

'Cherry! Come and take a selfie, over here!'

Cherry just smiled, waved and shook her head. She didn't want to make enemies but she also knew now that she didn't want to be like them. Cherry took a deep breath and walked over to Ruth and Joe, who were sitting on a bench.

Cherry stood in front of them awkwardly, looking at her feet. They carried on talking.

'Hi,' said Cherry quietly.

They turned and looked at her. There was a pause that seemed to Cherry to go on forever. She stared at the ground.

'Hey,' said Ruth.

Ruth and Joe glanced at each other. There was another long pause.

'Come and sit with us if you like. I'm Joe. We were just talking about our favourite movies.'

Cherry felt her cheeks flush. They were giving her another chance without any need for words and she sat down beside them gratefully. But what could she say? Cherry had never actually seen a film! There was no way she could tell them that, could she? They'd think she was a total idiot!

'Oh yeah,' Cherry said casually, 'I love movies.'

'Me too! What's your favourite?' asked Joe. He looked so interested.

'I… well… I like all different kinds of films, it's hard to pick just one…' She didn't want to lie but she was desperate for Ruth to like her again after what happened yesterday and she really wanted to be friends with Joe too.

'I'm massively into sci-fi, superhero movies, that kind of stuff.'

'Oh yeah. Absolutely. Me too,' bluffed Cherry. 'What about you Ruth?' She quickly tried to turn the conversation away from herself.

'I really love Japanese anime,' said Ruth enthusiastically, 'the animation has such a unique style and it…'

'Oh no, don't get her started on all that!' Joe jumped up. 'Right, movie night at my house, Friday night! Hot dogs, popcorn, the works! I'll check with my dad. I'm sure we can find something we all want to see without too much arguing!'

.Cherry glowed. 'That would be brilliant, thanks so much!' She felt Bud's wings beating with excitement. He was definitely a social butterfly.

The bell rang and they headed into school, ignoring the dirty looks from the Slick Girls as they walked past. Cherry also tried to ignore a nagging feeling inside her.

It was going to be hard to face Mrs Hemlock after the mirror episode, so Cherry hurried into class, resolving to keep her head down, do her work and hopefully go unnoticed. It was hard to concentrate though. Cherry couldn't wait to talk to Joe and Ruth again.

At lunchtime, Cherry sat with Ruth and Joe to eat their sandwiches. Flora had filled slices of home-baked brown bread with cheese from the market and crisp lettuce from the garden, with some radishes to nibble on the side. Cherry took a delicious bite.

'I love gaming too,' said Joe, 'I've just got to the top level of Super Rad Wipeout.'

Cherry had absolutely no idea what he was talking about but decided to go along with it again. She really wanted Joe to think she was cool.

'Love Super Rad.'

'You do?' Joe seemed slightly surprised.

'But I'm not very good, don't know much about it,' she said quickly, trying to cover herself.

'No worries! I'll show you how to get through the levels when you come over for movie night. There are some good tricks you can do when you parachute into the Bad Rad Forest that mean you can upgrade your armour and it gives you extra protection from the Wipeout Warriors. You'll go up the levels in no time.'

Cherry was totally lost. Bad Rad Forest? Wipeout Warriors? Still, she tried to sound convincing. 'Oh amazing, thanks…'

'It's so awesome you like Super Rad. Ruth's not into it at all, are you?'

Ruth rolled her eyes. 'Not my thing. Just don't get it.'

Cherry looked at her, admiring how Ruth could just be herself. She wished she didn't worry about what Joe and everyone else thought of her. But she did. She was enjoying having something to talk to Joe about too, even if it meant saying a few little fibs.

'I'll leave you to it,' said Ruth, 'I'm going back in.'

Cherry thought that she looked a little hurt, but quickly she dismissed it from her mind.

'Have you got Cyber City 2?' Joe was on a roll. This was clearly his favourite topic of conversation.

'Sure,' said Cherry.

'NO WAY! But that's just come out in the last few days!'

Cherry started to feel hot and uncomfortable but there was no turning back now. She just had to keep going, she was in too deep.

'I haven't played it yet.' She tried to sound breezy.

Joe jumped up. 'Will you bring it over on Friday? We can play it together! I've got the first one, but the graphics are supposed to be so much better on City 2. I read that there are mind-blowing new levels, the Devil's Dungeon and the

Secret Serpent Sewer!'

'Errr… yeah. I'll bring it over.' Her mind leapt ahead. She'd just pretend she'd forgotten it. It would be ok. 'We'd better go back in,' Cherry said feeling flustered, 'the bell's about to go.'

'I can't wait to play it. Friday is going to be so fun, thanks Cherry.' Joe was grinning at her.

She felt that knot in her stomach again.

That afternoon, Cherry couldn't concentrate on the lessons at all. Ruth was working hard and barely looked at her. She was relieved when it was time to go home, she needed to escape and have time think on her own. Walking out of school, Joe ran to catch up with her. He was still talking about the games.

They were so busy chattering, they forgot about Ruth who walked more slowly and couldn't keep up with them. Bud, who was very fond of Ruth, since she was the only person who might

be vaguely aware of his existence, flew out of Cherry's hair when Joe wasn't looking, and danced in her eyeline, pointing sharply with his antennae to Ruth behind them. Cherry swotted him away. She was too busy talking to Joe to be distracted by whatever Bud was on about now.

'Hey, are you playing tonight?'

'Of course I am,' said Cherry.

'Cool. Let me know when you're online and we can play Super Rad, it'll be sick!'

Cherry was stunned. She had no idea that could be done.

'Great!' She forced a smile as Joe waved and headed home. What was she going to do now?

# Lies

When Cherry got home, she ran straight up to her room and shut the door. When she finally came down for tea, she found her mum frantically dabbing at burning embers that had been spat out by the fire onto the rug again. She ran to help her. Bud zipped anxiously between them both, though he was still cross with Cherry for snubbing him earlier.

'Mum, you have to be careful! Cooking on that fire is a bit crazy you know!'

Flora laughed it off. 'Oh it's fine, Cherry, no harm done, just a bit smokey and a few burns on the rug, but the garden stew is extra tasty! Want some? You must be starving after school.'

They sat together on the sofa, digging into
the hot soup, packed with potatoes, carrots and
freshly picked spring greens. Cherry watched the
fire flicker in the hearth, frowning as she thought
about what to do about Joe.

'Are you ok, Cherry? You're very quiet.' Flora
could tell something was wrong.

Cherry didn't say anything. Suddenly there was
a strange noise outside. They put down their soup
and rushed to the window. It was the blossom tree.

They watched as each bough sagged again,

creaking heartbreakingly as they dropped a little further.

'Oh no!' whispered Flora desperately.

She turned to Cherry.

'What is it? What's happened?'

Cherry was staring at the tree.

'Cherry?'

Bud flew out flew out from her hair, and perched on her bowl. He pointed to Flora then looked at Cherry sternly.

'Alright, I'll tell her, you don't have to do that!' muttered Cherry.

'What was that, Cherry?'

'Nothing Mum. It's just that,' she took a deep breath, 'I wasn't completely honest Mum…'

'You mean you lied? Cherry, why did you do that? You know the blossom tree said you have to be honest to stay here!'

'I just wanted to…' Cherry gulped, 'I wanted to fit in Mum! I wanted to join in conversations with my friends so that they would like me. So I pretended I'd watched these films they were talking about. Then I said I played computer games and now I'm supposed to play online tonight, and I can't and they'll know I lied. That's why that's happened to the blossom tree again! It knows what I've done. But I'm just trying to fit in Mum!'

Cherry hung her head miserably. Flora put her arms around her and rocked Cherry gently, trying to fight off her own feeling of foreboding.

'Cherry, you're going to have to go back to school tomorrow and be honest, no matter how hard it is. Remember, you always have to be honest.'

'I'm so sorry. I'm letting you down. I didn't mean to do any harm, I really didn't.'

'Shhhh. Try not to worry Cherry.' Flora smoothed her hair gently. Bud dodged quickly out of the way just in time.

'What about the tree Mum?'

They both looked out into the garden. The tree looked as if it was dying before their eyes. Despite her mother hugging her close, Cherry was starting to feel scared. Bud crawled onto her cheek and kissed her softly with his wings.

# Truth

Cherry was dreading trying to explain to Joe and Ruth why she had made up those stories. Why was she always getting things wrong? Would Ruth forgive her again? She walked slowly across the schoolyard with her head down, going over in her mind what she would say. As soon as she had the chance, she would go straight up to Joe and Ruth. They were friends now, they would understand how she just wanted to fit in, to be like them, be liked by them. But she felt so different and she looked so different. Funny though, neither Ruth nor Joe had ever mentioned how she looked.

The class were already at their desks, books

open. Cherry was slightly relieved. At least it meant she didn't have to have that difficult conversation with Joe or Ruth right now.

'You're late, Cherry,' drawled Hemlock. 'Could we be bothered to come to school today?'

'Sorry, Mrs Hemlock,' said Cherry.

Hemlock seemed determined not to like her, but all that mattered to Cherry right now, were her friends. She glanced at Ruth next to her who smiled and mouthed 'don't worry' to her. Cherry turned around and saw Joe at the back of the class trying to catch her eye. He gave her a quick thumbs up then put his head down to do his work. She couldn't bear the thought of them not wanting to be friends with her any more.

Too quickly it was breaktime and Joe came bounding over to them.

'Hey Cherry! What happened last night? I thought you were up for some gaming?'

'I know. I'm sorry. Look, can I talk to you and Ruth? Let's go outside to our usual spot.'

They made their way across the playground to

their favourite bench. Cherry made sure she walked a little more slowly so that Ruth wasn't left behind. She desperately hoped this wasn't the moment she lost her only true friends. Suddenly, she knew what she had to do. She had to be totally and utterly honest. Not just about the lies she had told, but about who she really was, a flower girl, made by magic from blossom, but still, just a girl who needed friends. They may not believe her, and even Cherry had to admit it seemed a little far-fetched, but at least she would have told the truth. They would see her for who she really was and hopefully, they would still want to be her friends.

Ruth sat down next to them.

'Hey Cherry. You ok?'

Cherry took a deep breath. 'Not really. I'm so sorry. I've lied to you both. I don't know if I like movies, I've never seen one and I've never gamed.'

'What? You lied?' Joe's eyes were wide.

Ruth just looked at her. 'Why would you lie about that Cherry? It wouldn't matter to us either way.'

'But it does matter that you lied.' Joe was shaking his head.

'I know. I see that now. I was just so scared you wouldn't like me, I wanted to fit in. I mean, look at me, I'm so different to everyone else.'

'We're all different,' said Ruth. 'I sometimes wish I could walk and run like everyone else. I can't, but I just have to accept that. Tiffany and Amelia think it's weird I'm into nature and Japanese anime, but that's just me,' she shrugged.

'Yep and everyone knows I'm a total sci-fi geek!' said Joe happily.

'But you're a gamer. Everyone thinks that's cool!' exclaimed Cherry.

'Gaming geek. Sci-fi geek. I know way too much about all that stuff. But what about you? I know you've got the pink hair thing, but that's your choice, it doesn't mean you have to lie about stuff?' He sounded cross again.

She knew it was now or never and there was no easy way to say it.

'That's just it,' said Cherry. 'It's not a choice, this

is me. I was… made this way.' She took a deep breath. 'I was made from blossom by a cherry tree, that's why my hair is like this. I'm trying to do everything right so I can stay being a girl, but I just keep getting things wrong and then the tree gets sad and it's starting to die…' Her voice trailed off. Saying it out loud made her realise how fragile her life was and how brief it could be. She also realised how incredible her story sounded. How would they ever believe her?

The three of them sat in silence for a few seconds.

Then Joe exploded. 'That is the most ridiculous thing I've ever heard! I can't believe you expect us to believe that rubbish after you've already fed us a pack of lies! How stupid do you think we are? I was going to forgive you Cherry, and start over – yet again – but now this! You're just a liar!'

'No I'm not Joe, it's true, I promise…'

'True? You don't know the meaning of the word!' He leapt to his feet, hurt and angry. 'If you're some sort of blossom girl, prove it then! Show us!'

Cherry shook her head frantically, hoping for petals to fall to show them she was a flower girl, but nothing. Was it because she was so scared? Bud sensed her panic and shrank back into her curls. Desperately, Cherry clutched at her hair, willing petals to fall, but nothing. She tugged harder. Why wouldn't they come?

'Stop it! Stop it!' Ruth grabbed her arm. 'Don't Cherry, it's ok. Joe sit down!'

There was something in the tone of Ruth's voice that made them both listen. Joe sank down next to them, his head in his hands.

'I believe you, Cherry.'

Cherry and Joe both looked equally amazed.

'I saw,' said Ruth, 'I saw them when you cried. I saw your petal tears. Nobody can cry petal tears unless... unless they're made of blossom.'

Cherry threw her arms around her.

'Thank you for believing me. For seeing me.' Tears of relief and gratitude prickled in her eyes, and Joe saw two petals escape from beneath her eyelashes and float into the sky.

'Whooooaaah,' he shook his head, 'seriously? Actually made of blossom…?'

'I'm sorry I didn't tell you before,' she said, still hugging Ruth as two more petal tears fluttered into the breeze. Out of the corner of her eye, Cherry was aware of Bud crawling shyly from her hair and onto her cheek. He tilted his head to one side and looked, first at Joe and then at Ruth, giving her his most winning smile and a little wink.

'Oh yes. This is Bud, my butterfly. He seems to live in my hair.'

Bud wiggled his antennae and waved his wings at Ruth and Joe. Their jaws dropped open.

'Team hug?' said Cherry, 'and you too Bud.'

After quick, fluttery butterfly wing kisses for his new friends, he fluttered around the three of them and Cherry couldn't stop a few more petal tears escaping from her eyes.

As they let go of each other and drew away, Cherry saw Tiffany and Amelia staring at her.

They'd seen everything. She had a feeling this would not go well.

# Temper

'Like, what the slick is happening to your face? What are those things coming out of your eyes?' Tiffany looked disgusted.

'Yeah weirdo, what is that stuff, it's like, so gross!' sneered Amelia.

The girls started pretending to be sick, bending over and making loud retching noises.

The Slick Girls' dramatic performance attracted the attention of others in the playground, who stopped what they were doing and turned to look at them.

'She had all this pink gunk stuff coming out of her eyes, it was like, so grim.' Tiffany pretended she was going to be sick again.

'Yeah, it was so freakishly weird,' Amelia started retching again too.

'Just leave me alone,' whispered Cherry. There was no way she could even begin to explain the truth to these girls.

'You're such a freak Cherry!' Tiffany shouted.

'Yeah. Total weirdo!' Amelia chorused.

Bud swooped furiously at the two girls, but they barely noticed him.

'Please,' Cherry put her hands into her hair and tried to cover her ears, 'just leave me alone.'

She squeezed her eyes shut to try and stop any more petal tears.

'You heard her. Leave her alone, you idiots.' Ruth stood up.

'Shut up, Ruth' snarled Tiffany, 'you're just as freaky as she is!'

'Why don't you run off and take some more selfies?' Joe stood beside them too.

Bud settled on his shoulder in support and nodded hard.

'You can shut up, geek!' Amelia sneered at Joe.
Then they started chanting.

'Freaks! Freaks! Freaks!'

An unfamiliar feeling was welling up inside
Cherry.

'Stop it. Now,' she said through clenched teeth.

The Slicks ignored her and just chanted more
loudly.

'Freaks! Freaks! Freaks!'

The words were ringing in Cherry's ears and
their faces swam before her eyes.

'Freaks! Freaks! Freaks!'

'Ignore them, Cherry,' said Ruth calmly,
'they're just not worth it.'

But Cherry couldn't block them out. All her
pent up hurt and frustration of the past week had
been building up and now this attack, not just on
her, but on Ruth and Joe. It was too much.

'Freaks! Freaks! Freaks!'

It felt like an earthquake inside her and Cherry
began to shake uncontrollably.

'Freaks! Freaks! Freaks!'

She couldn't find the strength to hold herself back anymore. She had no control over this rising outrage and anger. How could they be so horrible to her friends?

Her arms shot out in front of her and, like a volcano erupting, from every fingertip, powerful jets of petals exploded from her.

Bud dived into her hair for cover.

The force of the petals sent Tiffany and Amelia staggering backwards, as streams of blossom bombarded them. Cherry's green eyes glowed like emeralds and Tiffany and Amelia were blasted to the ground, petals pelting them, mounting up over them. It was like they were being swallowed up whole by a hungry beast made of pink confetti.

'Stop! Stop it please! We're sorry! We're sorry!' The girls were chewing and spitting petals out of their mouths as they spoke, rolling around waving their arms and kicking their legs in the air, trying to stand but it was impossible.

Ruth reached out and touched Cherry's arm. Still the petals fired at the girls, the spraying

blossom buffeting them from all
sides.

'Cherry, enough,' said Ruth
firmly.

Cherry felt as if she was coming
out of a trance. She blinked
slowly and lowered her arms.

The petal shower slowly dripped
to a stop and the glow in her eyes faded.

'I… I don't know what happened…'

She looked at her hands as if they weren't her
own. The whole playground was staring at her,
mouths open. Tiffany and Amelia were still flailing
around in the petal pile.

'Get these things off me!' shrieked Tiffany.

'I'm stuck in them!' shouted Amelia, kicking her
legs in the air.

'Tiff, Amelia… I'm so sorry…'

Cherry felt a desperate sadness and shame
well up in her again. She hadn't been strong.
She had let her anger overcome her in the worst
possible way and she knew what this meant. It
had been another test, her final test, and she had
failed. Again. She had to get home. She had to get
back to her mother and to the blossom tree. Bud

crawled slowly out of Cherry's curls, his antennae drooping, wings sagging, his big eyes brimming with tears.

Cherry turned to Ruth and hugged her tightly.

'Thank you for everything,' she whispered. She turned to Joe. 'Thank you too. You've been the best friends I could have wished for.'

And with that, she turned and ran from the playground, sending a cloud of petals into the air behind her.

# Fire

Cherry ran out of the school gates, along the street and down into the park. Something was happening to her. She was starting to feel weak. She glanced down at her feet and legs as she ran. Petals were falling from them with each step. She glanced at her hands and arms, and saw pale pink blossom petals peeling from her skin. As they fell away from her, Cherry herself was starting to fade. She was dissolving into blossom once again. The petals had gained a life of their own. As they fell, they gathered together, following her purposefully back home, back to the blossom tree.

Cherry knew this was the end. She had failed.

Why couldn't she have been stronger? Losing her temper in that way, there could be no turning back. She would never see Ruth or Joe again. She wouldn't be a daughter. She let out a sob. She had to see her mother one last time, to say goodbye, to say how sorry she was.

A wind was gathering around her. Petals drifted from her hair. It was as if she was evaporating into the swirling air. She felt so weak, but forced herself to keep moving. She rounded the corner and her home at the edge of the park came into view.

Cherry stopped suddenly and gasped in horror.

There were clouds of smoke above the house and she could see flames licking the windows. Bud flew from her hair and hovered next to her face, his wings tense and quivering, his eyes wide and frightened.

Finding strength from somewhere, Cherry started running towards her home as fast as she could, Bud flying alongside her. That fire her mum cooked over was always spitting embers, had they set the house alight?

Her heart was thumping.

She knew Flora would be in there and she had to save her.

Cherry staggered to the side door which entered the garden, petals still peeling from her. She lurched past the failing blossom tree. A branch snapped and crashed to the ground. Cherry felt as if her heart cracked too, she was fading fast. That didn't matter now. It was over for her, but she needed to know her mother was safe.

Cherry pushed at the back door. The handle was hot and hurt her fingers, but gathering all her strength she swung it open and ran inside. The house was full of smoke, flames crackling at the windows and walls. Cherry could barely see. She tried to shout out but immediately started coughing.

'Mum!' she choked.

Where was she? Cherry's eyes strained through the smoke. Then suddenly she saw her, slumped on the floor in front of the fire.

'Mum!' Cherry groped her way through the

living room and dropped to her knees next to Flora. 'Mum! Wake up! Come on! You have to get out! Mum!'

Bud was covering Flora's face with butterfly kisses trying desperately to wake her, but she lay still. Cherry would have to drag her out.

She grabbed Flora's arms and pulled as hard as she could.

Flora barely moved.

Cherry pulled again but it was no use. She was so weak now, she couldn't move her.

'No!' sobbed Cherry. 'No!'

Petals were streaming from her eyes and shedding fast from her skin, she was vanishing into the smoke.

She lay her head on her mother's heart. 'I'm so sorry,' she whispered.

'Cherry!'

Distantly she heard a voice calling her name.

Was it Ruth?

'Cherry! Are you in there? Get out quick! The house is going to collapse!'

Yes, it was Ruth! And that was Joe!

Cherry felt a surge of energy. Her friends had come to help her, just as she had come to help her mother. She had to find a way, for all of them.

Through the grey ash in the air, Cherry could still make out her petals twitching in agitation above her. Bud swooped down and fluttered frantically in front of her face. With his antennae, he was pointing furiously at the petals around them. The petals? Yes, of course!

She had seen their power when they burst out of her, maybe this time she could control them.

She dragged herself upright.

'Petals!' The swirling stopped and they froze in mid-air, almost standing to attention. Could this actually work? 'Petals,' she gasped, 'pick up Mum! Pick up Flora!'

Immediately, millions and millions of blossom petals rushed to her mother. They surrounded Flora, lifting her into the air as if she were as light as a petal herself.

'Take her to safety,' she coughed, 'take her to

the blossom tree!'

Swiftly, they carried Flora on a soft stretcher of blossom out of the smoke-filled living room, through the back door and into the garden. They lay her down gently at the foot of the broken blossom tree, making themselves into a bed for Flora to lie on.

Cherry staggered out of the house and immediately fell to the ground. Bud flew down next to her and kissed her fading cheek with his wings.

Ruth and Joe rushed to her side. She was barely a girl at all now. The petals that had made her, had almost all drifted from her. She would soon disappear into a pink mist once again.

'Mum…' Cherry had to see her, make sure she was alive.

'We need to get her to her mum and the tree quickly!' said Ruth.

She and Joe lifted Cherry, even though she was drifting into petals in their hands, that floated through their fingers. They lay down the disappearing girl next to her mother.

'Mum…'

Flora opened her eyes. She could just make out the shimmering shape of her daughter, the light in her leaf-green eyes fading.

'Cherry… don't leave me…'

But Cherry was gone.

# The Gift

The petals that had surrounded Flora, that had made Cherry, soared into the air and once again, the garden was caught up in a pink storm. They twisted wildly, just as they had done before, and Flora looked up to see the face of the blossom. She spoke.

'Cherry has failed.'

Flora hung her head and nodded. 'I know our pact. Thank you for letting me be her mother, even just for a while. It was the most magical gift.'

Ruth and Joe held on to each other desperately. Their friend had just disappeared before their eyes. Bud had vanished too. The fire was still burning inside the house. Now a tree seemed to be speaking.

Joe elbowed Ruth. 'Is that blossom like, actually talking? And is it… looking at us?' Ruth gulped. 'I think so,' she said, eyes wide.

Flora's heart was breaking. She coughed hard, her lungs full of smoke, and closed her eyes. It was over. Cherry was gone. The blossom spoke again.

'She was not kind to Ruth, she was not honest with Joe, and she was not strong enough to control her temper…'

'I don't mind!' shouted Ruth, 'I don't care, please!'

'Yeah, it doesn't matter about the gaming thing!' Joe backed her up. 'I mean, yes of course I would have liked to have played Cyber City 2 because the new graphics are supposed to be…'

Ruth shot him a look and he stopped immediately.

The blossom smiled at Ruth and Joe and Flora.

'…But Cherry has shown she can be a kind friend and daughter. She learned to be honest about who she is and to admit when she is wrong. She may not have been able to control her temper with those mean girls, although I think even I may have struggled to with that pair!'

'Did the blossom just wink?' whispered Joe.

'Shhhhhh!' Ruth hissed.

The blossom continued.

'To be kind and honest, you must be strong. And it takes strength to love. Cherry has proved how much she loves you all. That love made her strong enough to stand up for her friends and it made her strong enough to save your life Flora. I believe, people who love each other, should be together.'

Flora opened her eyes and looked up slowly. Joe and Ruth drew their breath.

Could there be hope?

The smiling blossom face vanished into the cloud of petals. They began to churn, turning faster and faster, as the pink tornado surged in the garden once again. Flora shut her eyes while the petals hurtled around her. Ruth and Joe buried their heads into each other's shoulders.

Suddenly, all was still once more. Together, the three of them opened their eyes, not knowing what to expect. They could barely believe what they saw.

The house was just as it had been. There was no sign of the fire. The blossom tree was in full bloom, powdery blossom weighing heavily on every single branch. Standing beneath it, beaming the biggest grin, was Cherry with a pink butterfly dancing crazily on the top of her head. She dropped to her knees next to Flora.

'Hi Mum,' she whispered.

Flora sobbed and flung her arms around her. Ruth and Joe threw themselves on top of them too, hugging Flora and Cherry as Bud whizzed around them.

'Cherry…' said Flora, crying and laughing at the same time, 'do you think you could introduce me to your friends?'

# Back to school

It was difficult going to school after what had happened.

Cherry went straight to see the head teacher to try to explain, but Miss Turner looked extremely puzzled as Cherry tried to tell her all about losing her temper and flying petals.

'I don't quite know what you're trying to say, Cherry,' she boomed, 'but well done for coming to see me. Can't have been easy. Whatever happened, you're clearly sorry and that's what matters to me. Let's get you straight back to class.'

Cherry was so relieved.

Miss Turner strode out of her office and Cherry

walked nervously behind her as she marched down the corridor and straight into a noisy classroom.

At the sight of the head, the children stopped chattering and sprung to their desks. Cherry shuffled into the room, knowing that her outburst had probably been the main topic of their conversation.

'Cherry has told me what happened yesterday and she has apologised. Could have happened to anyone. Well, I say anyone, maybe not quite anyone, but that's not the point. This school is accepting and it is forgiving, so we move on and I don't want to hear another word about it, is that clear?'

'Yes, Miss Turner,' the class said back in unison.

'Cherry take your seat.'

Cherry scuttled quickly, like a nervous beetle, to get to her desk. As she walked past Tiffany and Amelia, Tiffany reached out and grabbed her arm. Cherry jumped, but Tiffany gently released her grasp and she and Amelia looked up at Cherry.

The girls nodded in unison, smiled briefly, then, perfectly in time with each other, turned back to their books.

Cherry took a deep breath. Everything was going to be alright.

Miss Turner, satisfied, strode out of the room.

'Good morning class.' Mrs Hemlock had arrived.

'Good morning Mrs Hemlock,' they chanted slowly.

'I think today would be a good day to do some creative writing. It appears you are all rather good at imaginative stories,' she said dryly, looking pointedly at Cherry, 'so let's get to work shall we?'

Cherry picked up her pencil and opened her workbook, glanced at Ruth and they grinned secretly at each other. How could they even begin to make up a story that was more exciting than their own real adventure?

# Movie Night

It was Friday night, movie night at Joe's. Cherry couldn't wait to go to his house and hang out with her friends. He didn't live far away, but her mum wanted to walk over with her, just to be safe.

After school, Flora and Cherry baked shortbread biscuits to take as a gift for Joe and his dad. They cut them into flower shapes and together, decorated them with pale pink icing so they looked like blossom flowers. Flora wrapped them up in brown paper but the sweet, buttery smell wafted out, making Cherry's mouth water.

'Let's go, Mum!' Cherry was practically pulling Flora out of the house and ten minutes later, they were standing outside the forest-green door of Joe's house. Cherry knocked enthusiastically.

Joe's dad opened it almost immediately.

'Hi! We've baked biscuits for you.' Cherry announced proudly.

'That's so kind of you. Wow, they smell good! Great to see you both, come in, come in. I've heard lots about you Cherry.' His eyes flickered up towards her hair as Bud popped out and came eye to eye with Joe's dad, whose jaw was now gaping open. Bud gave him a quick wink and dived back into Cherry's hair. 'Ch… Cherry, I think there was something… in your hair…'

Joe's dad looked very confused.

Joe and Ruth appeared just in time, so Cherry didn't have to try and answer.

'Stop being embarrassing dad!' Joe rolled his eyes but was smiling. 'Come on Cherry, let's go into the garden.'

'Right, what film are we going to watch?' asked Joe.

He wanted a space movie, Star something or other that Cherry had never heard of. Joe and Ruth couldn't believe she didn't know it but Cherry just giggled and didn't try to pretend anything this time.

Cherry looked again at her mum laughing with Joe's dad in the kitchen. She turned to Ruth and Joe who were sitting next to her, still winding each other up about their movie choices. She felt like the luckiest girl in the world. She had loyal friends, a loving mother, and now, she was truly alive.

Gradually, Cherry became aware Ruth and Joe had stopped talking and were looking at her.

'Yes, can I help you?' she asked, trying to sound funny, but it looked like Ruth was about to say something serious.

'Cherry,' Ruth said hesitantly, 'you know the whole petal thing?'

'Oh yeah, right, that was so cool!' exclaimed

Joe, 'like whooosshhh…' He shot his arms out in front of him, firing imaginary jets of petals around the garden.

Ruth rolled her eyes. Cherry smiled, but she still felt ashamed that she'd lost her temper with Tiffany and Amelia.

Ruth carried on.

'You know when you get the petals to do things? I just wondered… can you do that whenever you want?'

'I don't know,' said Cherry honestly. 'I'm not even sure how it happens, it just bursts out sometimes.' She thought about when the petals had appeared. 'I suppose maybe it's when I really feel strongly about something. When I'm cross, when I'm scared, or…'

A thought struck her. She looked at her friends who had stood by her through everything. Maybe…

'Come here.' Cherry stood up and held out her hands. 'Join hands in a circle. Let's spin.'

They held each other's hands tightly and

started to move. Bud fluttered around them, wondering what on earth Cherry was up to now.

'Faster!' said Cherry and her hair flew out behind her as they picked up speed.

'I'm so dizzy!' shouted Ruth laughing.

'I'm going to fall over!' yelled Joe.

Cherry closed her eyes, smiling. She felt the sun on her face, her friends' hands in hers and thought of her mother's kindness. She had more than she could ever have wished for. As she felt a surge of love, petals burst from her, springing out from the curls of her hair. Out they poured, tumbling over each other to race to freedom. The friends whirled faster and faster like a spinning wheel, weaving more and more petals from Cherry's blossom hair.

'You've done it, Cherry!' gasped Joe.

'They're so beautiful! It's incredible!' said Ruth in wonder.

Cherry felt another rush of tenderness towards her friends and the shimmering swirl of petals wrapped around them more closely like layers of feather-light ballerina's tulle, gracefully binding

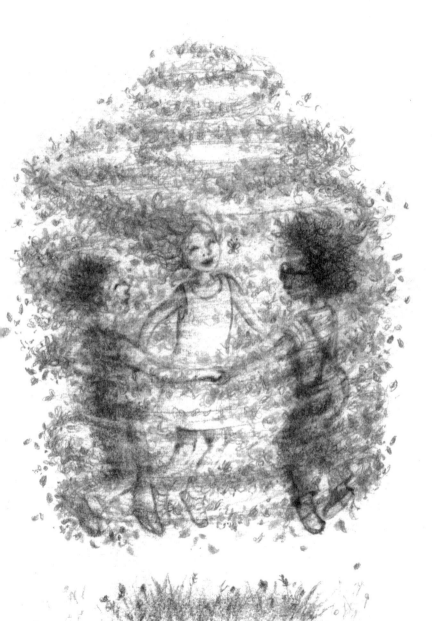

them together. Then suddenly, a powerful pirouette of pink petals surged together and lifted them right off the ground!

'Whoooaahhh!' Joe couldn't believe it.

'Are we flying?' said Ruth incredulously, 'it feels like we're flying Cherry!'

Higher they rose, into the evening air, the pale blue sky now sparkling and sequinned with pink petals.

Bud was so excited that his friends were finally flying like him, he dived in to ride the jet stream on wild wings.

They were weightless, twirling, round and round like wisps of candy floss on a stick.

The sun broke through the petal cloud and it glittered like sugar crystals, dazzling and sparkling, a treasure chest of pink diamonds emptied into the sky.

Time itself had stopped. There was only this pure moment.

The three friends squeezed each other's hands, sharing the magic together. They breathed in deeply and it was as if their hearts were beating as one.

Together, the petals were strong enough to do anything, and so were these friends, bonded forever by a flower girl.

The petals lowered them softly to the ground. All three stood frozen, barely able to believe what had just happened. Then Joe and Ruth burst into life and threw themselves onto Cherry, hugging her tightly. She squeezed them back, until the dizziness hit them all and they collapsed onto the ground laughing.

The petals dumped themselves heavily around them, exhausted by their effort. They rose lightly and fell again, sighing contentedly, casting their warm, pearly glow over the friends.

A bedraggled Bud, looking as if he'd just come off the world's biggest rollercoaster, flopped into the bed of Cherry's cotton wool hair.

'How did you do that Cherry?' breathed Ruth.

Cherry shook her head. 'I'm still not entirely sure,' she said slowly, 'but, I think it may happen when…' she hesitated shyly.

'When what?' asked Joe.

'Well, when I'm just…' she paused again.

Ruth reached out for her hand. Bud fluttered up and kissed Cherry's cheek with a brush of his wings. He perched on the tip of her nose and wiggled his antennae eagerly, encouraging her to answer. A smile grew on Cherry's lips, blossoming into a huge grin.

'Come on, Cherry!' giggled Ruth, nudging her.

'Yes, what's the secret or do I have to tickle it out of you?' Joe was getting ready to go for her feet.

'Ok, ok! No tickling!'

Cherry took a deep breath. 'The magic secret?'

'Yes?' Ruth's eyes, Joe's eyes and Bud's eyes were all wide in anticipation.

'It's quite simple actually, just not always that easy…'

Bud had now zoomed into air, and was hovering next to Ruth and Joe, quivering and twitching, barely able to stand the suspense of a secret about to be shared.

Cherry giggled. 'It's ok Bud. Honestly, I think it's just being…'

'CHERRY? WHAT?' Joe and Ruth chimed together.

'Happy!' smiled Cherry simply.

And millions of pink petals surged into the sky.

# Cherry's Picks

Hi, I'm Cherry!

I hope you enjoyed reading my story. It's pretty fun being made from blossom, so I thought you might like to know a little bit more about these beautiful trees and about my story. I've cherry-picked a few facts for you.

## 1

There's another girl I've read about who is made of flowers. Her name is Blodeuwedd (you say it Blod-ay-with). Her name literally translates as 'flower face'! She is written about in the *Mabinogion*, which is a collection of ancient Welsh stories.

## 2

Legend says Blodeuwedd was made from nine types of flower. Here we go! Some flowers were from an oak tree, some were from a shrub called broom, which often has yellow flowers. She's made from a herb with heart-shaped leaves called burdock. Blooms from bean plants, nettles, chestnuts, primroses, and hawthorn flowers all come together to make her. And the last plant is meadowsweet, a herb with fluffy white cloud-like flowers. Phew! That's a lot of different flowers for one girl, not like me who's just cherry blossom!

## 3

Cherry blossoms are Japan's national flower and are very special to people there. They are a symbol of spring, a time when nature comes alive again. But trees don't flower for long. It takes about a week for the blossom to reach full bloom, then a week later, petals start to fall from the trees.

Because the flowering is so brief, in Japan they are said to be a reminder that our lives are fragile and the blossom's beauty should make us remember how beautiful life is too.

## 4

In Japan, cherry blossom trees are called 'sakura'. When they bloom, there is a tradition of having parties beneath them. The custom is called 'hanami', which literally means 'watching blossoms'. It sounds fun. I'm going to ask Mum if we can have a party under our cherry tree!

## 5

Did you like the idea of the patchwork quilt that Flora made? There is a long tradition of quilting in Wales, dating back hundreds of years. Welsh quilts are known for their striking, simple designs. People would buy bags of scraps of old material to make them. One of the most wonderful quilts I've heard of is The Wrexham Tailor's Quilt from 1842! It's at St Fagans National Museum of History in Cardiff. It has animals and birds, even a whale, embroidered onto it and it took a whole ten years to sew! Phew!

## ∽ 6 ∾

Ruth loves Japanese animation. It's called 'anime' and has a very distinctive style. Because the cherry tree is so important to people in Japan, it is often seen in anime. I can't wait to watch some of those films with Ruth.

## ∽ 7 ∾

The National Trust is going to be planting lots of blossom trees across the UK! The charity hopes that their beauty will bring happiness and that the natural spaces they create will be places of hope and reflection. Trees of every kind are really important for our planet. The National Trust want to plant 20 million of them in the years to come. Wow!

## 8

My mum works very hard in her garden and to grow all her vegetables. I'm learning to grow things now too. I've started with lettuces and carrots, which are supposed to be really easy. You don't need to have a garden either! You could even start by just growing herbs in pots! Why don't you give it a try?

## 9

Ruth has difficulty walking because she has a condition called cerebral palsy. It affects how you move and your co-ordination. It happens if a baby's brain doesn't develop normally in their mum's tummy or if a baby doesn't get enough oxygen from the air when it's born. Sometimes it is because a baby is born early and is not ready to cope with being outside their mummy's tummy. Some people, like Ruth, only have minor problems. Others can have more severe disabilities. The type of cerebral palsy Ruth has is called hemiplegia where one side of her body does not move as well as the other.

There is currently no cure for cerebral palsy, but there are treatments to help people be as active and independent as possible. Ruth gets help from a wonderful charity in Wales. You can find out more about them here: cerebralpalsycymru.org.

## ⤾10⤿

Shall we have some fun imagining and creating together? Let's think… if you could be made from any flower, which flower would you pick? What would you look like? What special power might you have? You could draw a picture or write your own story and share it with your family, friends, teachers – and me please! I would love to say hello to flower friends everywhere.

Thank you for reading my story.
Love, Cherry x

lucyowenbooks.com
rebeccaharry.com

# Flora's Fabulous Feasts

You may have noticed when you were reading my story that my mum makes really delicious meals and treats. They are so yummy!

Now she's helping me learn to cook. Do you like cooking? If you'd like to learn with me, here are some of her tasty recipes to try.

Have fun!
Love, Cherry x

# Flora's Easy-Peasy Gloriously Green Veggie Soup

- A glug of olive oil
- 2 sticks of celery
- 2 cloves of garlic
- 2 leeks
- 2 courgettes
- 100g of frozen or fresh peas
- 250g of broccoli
- 1 litre of veggie or chicken stock
- Salt and pepper
- A few basil leaves
- Your favourite bread for dunking!

- Have some fun chopping your veggies into bite-sized chunks. Ask a grown-up to help if you need to use a sharp knife. You could try using scissors if you like.

- Heat the oil gently in a big saucepan.
- Put in the leeks, celery and garlic and let them cook until they are soft.
- Add the courgettes, broccoli and peas and cook for about 5 more minutes. Stir things up from time to time.
- Add your veggie or chicken stock to the pan – either would be lovely.
- Season with salt and pepper and let it all simmer away for about 10-15 minutes.

### Flora's top tip!

You could add a handful of pasta, rice or shredded cooked chicken if you wanted to at this point.

- When all your glorious vegetables are cooked, there's nothing left to do apart from let it cool slightly, ready to enjoy. A few basil leaves or a swirl of natural yoghurt would make this a super special supper. A sprinkling of your favourite cheese would be delicious too.

# Flora's Rhubarb Crumble

The Filling
- 900g of rhubarb
- 2 tbsp of runny honey
- 1 orange, juiced and zested
- 35g of caster sugar

The Crumble
- 100g of plain flour
- 50g of ground almonds
- 125g of chilled, unsalted butter (cut into cubes)
- 70g of demerara or caster sugar
- Pinch of salt

- Preheat your oven to 200°C /180°C fan/gas mark 6.
- Cut the rhubarb into approximately 3cm slices and put them in a medium-sized baking dish.

- Mix together the sugar, orange juice and zest and honey. Plop this mixture onto the rhubarb and mix it all together.
- Now it's time to get a bit messy. In a big bowl mix together all your crumble topping ingredients. Make sure your hands are squeaky clean and then, using your fingertips, rub the butter into all the dry ingredients until they look a bit like slightly lumpy breadcrumbs.
- Sprinkle the crumble mix over your fruit. At this point you can go a bit wild and add some extras like granola, oats, choc chips or nuts, which would all be lovely.
- Pop the dish in the oven for 35-40 minutes or until golden and bubbling.

It's probably best to ask a grown-up to take it out of the oven.

- Leave to cool for about 10 minutes. Now...
  spoon it into your favourite bowl with plenty
  of custard or ice cream or even a bit of both...
  why not!

These recipes have been designed by a real-life
Flora who lives outside the pages of this book.
You can order her cakes and treats through
Instagram @foodwithflora and have something
special made just for you.


They are also available from:
Forage Farm Shop and Kitchen, Penllyn Estate,
Llwynhelig, Cowbridge, Vale of Glamorgan
CF71 7FF
www.foragefarmshop.co.uk
And
Arboreal Café Kitchen Bar, 68 Eastgate Street,
Cowbridge CF71 7AB
www.arboreal.uk.com

# Bek's Blossom Biscuits

Biscuits
- 175g of plain flour
- 100g of butter cut into cubes
- 50g of caster sugar
- 1 egg yolk
- ¼ tsp of vanilla extract
- about 2 tsp of water

Icing
- 350g of royal icing sugar
- about 3 tsp of water
- Pink food colouring

⤳ To make the biscuits: ⤳

- Preheat oven to 190°C /170°C fan/gas mark 5.
- Sift the flour into a mixing bowl. Add the butter and rub in until the mixture looks like fine breadcrumbs. Then mix in the caster sugar.

- Make a well in the centre and drop in the egg yolk. Add the vanilla extract and a teaspoon of water. Bring the mixture together with your hands to form a soft dough. Add a little more water if you need to. Cover it and chill for 30 minutes.
- Line 2 baking sheets with greaseproof paper.
- Roll out the dough on a lightly floured work surface to about 5mm thick.
- Using a flower cookie cutter, cut out your biscuit shapes as close together as possible. Trimmings can be re-rolled. Carefully pick up each biscuit with a palette knife and place on to the lined trays. The biscuits will spread a little when cooking so be sure to space them out.
- Bake for 10-12 minutes until pale golden.
- Allow to cool on the baking sheet for a few minutes then transfer to a wire rack to cool completely.

## Icing the biscuits:

- Mix royal icing sugar with water until thick and smooth.
- Carefully add pink colouring and stir well. Put half in a bowl and cover for later. This will be your flooding icing.

- Put the other half of the icing into a piping bag and pipe the outline of a flower on each biscuit. Leave to dry for 10 minutes at room temperature.
- Uncover your flooding icing and add enough water to make it a pouring consistency. Put into a clean icing bag.
- Now flood each biscuit with pink icing up to your outline edge.
- Place the biscuits on to a baking tray until the icing has set hard.
- You can add more detail to the centre of the flower at this point using different coloured piped icing.

## Enjoy your blossom biscuits!

This biscuit recipe has been designed by Rebecca Harry, so these are actually Bek's blossom biscuits! Bek drew all the wonderful illustrations to go with my story. It turns out that she's not only really good at painting and drawing, she makes beautiful biscuits too!

# Acknowledgements

The most heartfelt thanks to Atebol for publishing this book and for making it such a totally joyous experience. Owain Saunders-Jones, your calm confidence and unwavering support have meant the world. Thank you for enabling Rebecca and I to work together again.

I feel like the luckiest writer ever to have had Super Editor Rach, occasionally known as Rachel Lloyd, devote her exceptional talent to *Flower Girl*. Thank you for understanding everything I tried to do with this little story, for your insight and remarkable attention to detail, and for generally making it so much better! It's been wonderful working with such an absolutely brilliant and lovely person. Kind, honest and strong – you're the Cherry on the cake!

Bek. Your illustrations *are* the book. They are so beautiful they make me cry, and only a truly beautiful person could create such magic. Thank you for everything.

Janet Thomas, you read a very early draft of the book and were so kind and encouraging. Thank you for helping me to move it forward.

Wonderful Eloise Williams, you champion us all, writers and readers. Thank you for everything you do, you are such a generous spirit. I have no doubt that during your time as Children's Laureate you have inspired children across Wales and made a real difference. Thank you for reading *Flower Girl*, I couldn't stop smiling after your lovely, kind words.

To the real-life Flora, who also happens to be the most brilliant cook! Thank you so much for contributing those delicious recipes and for being as sweet as the cakes you bake. I know children and their parents will really enjoy making – and eating! – these yummy treats.

Thank you to centre director and consultant physiotherapist Jenny Carroll at Cerebral Palsy Cymru for helping make sure I give the best portrayal of Ruth. This is the very first charity I became an ambassador for more than 25 years ago now, and it will always be very special to me.

I want to thank children's writers, bloggers, reviewers, publishers and Twitter friends. It feels such a privilege to be part of this warm and supportive writing and publishing community where everyone pulls together and looks after each other. Thanks for inviting me in.

To my family, friends, and colleagues, I'm eternally grateful to have such wonderful people in my life, who bring me more love and happiness every day than I deserve. Thank you.

And finally, thank YOU for taking time to read this book. I hope with all my heart you've enjoyed it. Like Cherry, be happy and let your petals fly!

Lucy x